SPY JEWEL

KELLI VANBRUNT

Order this book online at www.trafford.com
or email orders@trafford.com

Most Trafford titles are also available at major online book retailers.

Printed in the United States of America.

ISBN: 978-1-4669-8508-7 (sc)
ISBN: 978-1-4669-8510-0 (hc)
ISBN: 978-1-4669-8509-4 (e)

Library of Congress Control Number: 2013905395

Trafford rev. 03/27/2013

 www.trafford.com

North America & international
toll-free: 1 888 232 4444 (USA & Canada)
phone: 250 383 6864 ♦ fax: 812 355 4082

CHAPTER 1

Clover walked her bike up to the bike park. She took a deep breath. This was what she'd been waiting for, her fourteenth birthday, and the day of the challenge. Clover mounted her bike and pushed off. She pedaled faster than ever before toward the dip; her black, rubbery bike tires rolling smoothly across the cream-colored cement ground. She felt a shudder claw its way through her whole body as she neared the dip, and when she got there, the bike soared through the fresh, crisp late summer air for about a millisecond before it dropped. Clover steered the bike to the other side, feeling her slow down, and turned the bike around.

She let momentum carry her to the other side, where she again had to pedal a little to keep the bike gliding along. Duala watched from the four rows of shiny metal bleachers, every once in a while shouting encouragement to Clover.

Clover pedaled a bit too hard on her fifth turn, though, and it sent her flying into the other side. Duala hurried to help her friend, her ballet flats crunching through the brittle leaves that had fallen from an aspen grove, but Clover simply looked exasperated. "I wanted to turn ten times in a row. Either that, or break a leg."

Now Duala was exasperated.

The next day, the friends visited Maple's Gem Store. A sign was put up on the window:

WILL REWARD $50,000 IF YOU FIND A DIAMOND STOLEN FROM MAPLE'S GEM STORE!

Then there was a picture of the diamond. Duala turned her head, caught a twinkle in Clover's eye, and groaned. Clover pushed open the door to ask about the diamond.

"Why, anyone can find the diamond. If your parents agree, of course you can try and find it," Maple said, the corners of her cherry red lips turning up in a pleased smile, after Clover asked if she could try to find the diamond. "But you will probably want to have a starting place. I would recommend New York City, San Francisco.

As much as she tried to convince herself that she wouldn't be dragged into this by Clover, Duala imagined the two of them going to Mexico and possibly even Europe to find the precious diamond. "No, I won't," she whispered. What if she got Clover killed like her mother had been killed?

Duala, when she was three, had cracked a code her parents couldn't figure out. Her parents had been surprised and had enrolled her in a highly rated school, which was where she got her huge brain.

Duala had been going on adventures all around the world since she was four, and she had a clean and polished mind. If you were to look inside you would find organized stacks of things all over the place, and Duala's room was no different. Clover was reckless, even though the farthest from home she'd ever been was in the doctor's office. Her mind was messy, with the most important things stowed at the back and the details she didn't need in front. Her room was nicknamed the "Black Hole" because it was rumored that once you went in, you couldn't find your way out.

The first adventure Duala had ever had was right after she cracked the code. One day, on the tenth of April, her dad arrived from India, where he'd been working on a top-secret case. He couldn't even tell Duala about it, but he'd showed her a gold disk he'd found with numbers and letters on it in a circular pattern. The next day she noticed a word on the disc—"bring"—from the outer end of the disc to the inner end. She looked for words like this and found them—sometimes they were diagonal, sometimes scrambled, but they always went from the outer end to the inner end.

She showed her dad the sentences she'd figured out. Her dad had been proud and brought her on his next case, a baffling one where Duala wasn't as much help as the last one. Nevertheless, she enjoyed it very much.

Her mother loved her possibly more than her father, and because of that she insisted on going with the pair to a case that nearly got Duala and her dad killed. They'd been in a cave-in, and Duala's mother wasn't fast enough to escape the biggest boulder that crashed down. Duala swore that day that she would never go on a case again.

Clover's mom died in a way that was much more painful. She had lung cancer and didn't know it until it had spread, but then it was too late. She also had several heart attacks, each one more serious than the last.

Duala and Clover were chatting in line at the Malt Mall, the ice cream bar five miles downtown from Duala's place. "I'll have a chocolate chip ice cream, please," Clover ordered from the black-haired Asian cashier at the counter once they got to the front of the line.

"And you?" the cashier asked Duala.

"I'll have the same," Duala replied.

While they sat down to enjoy their food, Duala's mind wandered to the case of the stolen diamond. "Where do we go to find the diamond, Clover?"

"Let's start in New York. My aunt who lives in New York invited me to visit her. She said I could bring one friend, so I'll bring you," Clover said. She fiddled with her tangled red bangs nervously. Clover was scared of airplanes.

Duala smiled and reached out to touch her friend's freckle-covered hand comfortingly. Then she drew her hand back and thought of a million things that could go wrong—what if she was killed? What if she broke her leg? She fiddled with her glossy, brown locks and dipped one end in her ice cream.

After the evening at the ice cream bar, Clover went to Duala's house for a slumber party. Clover had asked all her other friends to come ("It's going to be the most fabulous party in history!" she said), including Kimberly, Sara, and Madeline.

Clover and Duala filled glass goblets with grape juice. They were the hostesses of the party. They set them on the table where the guests would be, and Clover tossed five gold-ringed china plates onto the spots. "What are we going to do tonight?" she asked.

"Duh! We're going to dance, and eat, and—"

"No, I mean when we get our sleeping bags out."

"Sleep, of course!"

"We won't, no matter how hard we try. This juice is the only stuff you have in the house, other than tap water, and I'm not drinking that. Juice makes you frizzy." That was what Clover called "energetic," "hyper," or whatever word you used that would describe being "over-energetic."

"I'll get out the feather pillows for the pillow fights!"

"You do that, Duala. I'll go over to the ice cream truck and ask if they can stop by at four. 'Kay?" Clover asked, getting a nod in return.

"We should put up a disco ball," Duala said to herself. She started looking for one, but two minutes later, Clover barged into the room, her red bangs dripping with sweat and her new yellow sneakers ("Yellow is so yesterday,"

Duala had said when she'd seen them) thudding against the carpeted floor. She'd obviously run as hard as she could to catch the truck.

"He said yes!"

Duala walked across the soft, forest-green carpet to a wooden closet door. She pulled it open with her right hand. "Aha!"

A dusty old ball coated with so much dust that you could barely see the little silver squares attached to it tumbled out of a box. That was the disco ball. "Duala, you finish hanging this sign up and I'll get the duster," Clover said. She hopped off of the stepladder and handed the hammer and the nails to Duala.

Five minutes later, the guests arrived.

"I'm here!" Sara shouted as she barged into the room without knocking. Sara was dressed in a blue, glittery party dress that hung just over her knees, reflecting light everywhere you could see. She lugged a light blue backpack over her shoulder. "Maybe *I* could be the disco ball instead!"

"How did you know we were planning on a disco ball?" Duala asked.

"Um, you do know Clover's carrying it, right?"

"Oh. Right."

Now Kimberly walked in. She was in a pink silk dress that trailed out of the door. A black velvet ribbon was tied around her waist. Red ballet flats were on her feet, and they were clearly new shoes. "*Bonjour,* girls. I'm signed up to be a babysitter! I'll have the most delicate little girl to babysit. She even takes ballet."

6

"Cool, Kimberly. Maybe when we have the disco ball ready, you can dance for us. You have to get ready for your recital, anyway," Duala said, just as a blonde girl in blue sneakers walked in.

"What's up, people? I brought my new soccer ball, hockey stick, and tennis racket. What are we playing?" Madeline, who wasn't really the feminine type but was prettier than any other girl in the room, asked the minute she stepped in the room.

"I was thinking we should head over to the pool. I brought my suit, and a few extra ones for you, guys. We could stay at the recreation center till four thirty, since it's four right now," Sara said.

"We should go to the ice skating rink. The most beautiful dancing is on the ice," Kimberly said, and sighed a long sigh.

"I vote for the field. Who's up for soccer?" Madeline asked.

"Actually, guys, we're having ice cream right now!" Clover exclaimed, rushing into the room with five already melting ice cream cones in her hands. "Chocolate for Duala and I, strawberry for Kimberly, bubble gum for Sara, and vanilla for Madeline."

At one o'clock in the morning, in her black leather sleeping bag, covered with soft, white feathers, frizzy wet hair, grass, and ice, Duala envisioned herself in New York. It was a pleasant sight. Duala had always wanted to go to New York.

When the plane ride came, Duala got exciting news on her cell phone—the police had found out that one of the thieves was heading south, and they were tracking him—or her—down. Duala told Clover about it.

Duala and Clover were driven to Durango, where the airport was, in Duala's dad's old red Mercedes. They departed in a crowded airplane. At one point during the flight, Duala saw that they were between two layers of clouds. She started taking picture after picture of the scene outside. The one-hour flight was long and tiring, and by the time they reached Denver, Duala was sleeping soundly. Clover had to shake her by the shoulders to get her to wake up.

On their next flight, this time to New York City, Clover looked at the man sitting across the aisle. His eyes were closed, and a blue velvet pouch sat on his lap, just small enough to fit into the palm of a child's hand. *That probably holds coins*, Clover thought, but then her gaze ventured to the man's back jeans pocket. A brown wallet was in it. Quarters, pennies, and dimes spilled out. She wondered what could be in the pouch, since all his coins were probably in the wallet.

Just then, the plane twisted and turned violently. They turned right and dropped, turned left and rose. Then the plane turned to the right and everything was back to normal. "I guess we're going around the thunderstorm," Duala said to Clover. The three-hour flight turned into a three-and-a-half hour flight.

Clover asked Duala, "Do you know anybody who stores anything in tiny pouches that could just barely fit into, say, the palm of an eight-year-old?"

"Yes, my aunt Florence. I just call her Auntie. She has something like a jewelry pouch. It's just about that size, and she puts really valuable things like rubies and emeralds in it. Once she had a piece of jade. Why do you ask?" Duala inquired.

Clover told Duala about the man, and when Duala said, "It could hold coins," Clover pointed out the wallet in the pocket. Soon, Duala was nodding and exclaimed, "It could hold the diamond!" at the end of their conversation. Duala made a note of his features on a piece of paper:

Goatee, brown hair slightly gray, mustache, dark tan skin, and long and skinny head.

The plane finally landed.

The man got out before the girls, and once the friends had gotten out, the man was nowhere to be seen. Clover noticed out of the corner of her eye that there was a window in the airport with a small fuzzy pouch propped up against it, identical to the one the man had.

The girls hurried toward the airport. "I wonder what's inside that bag. It looks pretty small, and not even enough to hold some money. I suppose it could be holding coins, but the man with that pouch has coins inside his wallet . . . let's go find out and see if somebody picks it up. I have a feeling this is worth investigating," Clover said.

"We should follow any reasonable leads," Duala agreed.

They waited on the platform next to the luggage cart. Finally a large hand picked up the pouch gingerly, as if it were a piece of gold. The hand left the window. Then, in a matter of seconds, a body burst out of the door. He got into a red convertible, and dropping a small object in it, he stepped on the gas.

Clover took out a ring from her pocket. She and Duala walked over to the parking lot inconspicuously. Clover looked around to make sure nobody was looking, then twisted the gemstone on it 180 degrees to the right. She let the ring drop, and it formed into a bike that looked like a common, everyday one with a single difference—it was painted the color gold. Even its tires were gold, and its back wheel had a giant green stone on it. This was the M&M (Magical and Multifunctional) bike.

The girls started pedaling. From the back wheel a tube emerged. The tube emitted a roaring sound, and they shot forward just like a rocket. Clover redirected the tube to guide them up, using the control pad on the handles. They shot upward and the tube slowly vanished into the back wheel. They were only airborne for a few moments before they fell. The bike's wheels deflated and spread so that it acted and looked like a giant glider. Duala turned on her electric screen that pinpointed where they were on the map of the street and saw that they were too high off the ground for her screen to receive signal. She sighed. Sometimes even high-tech bikes could be *so* demanding. Telling Clover to lower the bike, Duala saw on the screen that they were right above the Ford behind the man's convertible. Clover lowered the bike even more, making it turn to the right. Luckily, there was a field right by the street. The girls flew into that and they turned the bike back to the ring by pressing on the gemstone. The bike fell, and all of its features shrank into the back wheel. The wheel itself shrank too, and the girls fell to the ground, their knees bending and their bodies absorbing the impact as the ring clattered to the street.

Duala put a mini-telescope to her ear and dropped down. She could hear most of the men's conversation from here with her earscope. Depending on how far you stretched it, it could magnify sounds thousands of times until it rang in your ears. If you stretched it to its limit, you could hear snow hitting the ground. With an earscope stretched halfway to its limit, the beat of a hummingbird's wings would sound like an extremely loud rock band. Duala did not stretch the earscope even a bit. The words that the men were saying were clear as day.

" . . . Diamond?" one man asked, whispering.

"Safe and sound," the other man replied.

The girls stared at each other, wide-eyed. Clover's jade-colored eyes looked like giant emeralds, and Duala's eyes, both extremely pale grays, could have almost passed for moons.

The two crawled forward, ready to follow the men.

Clover cried out as she stepped in a hole and sprained her ankle. Realizing what she'd just done, both Clover and Duala fell to the ground and crawled up against a person's car. The man wasn't convinced and got out of his car to investigate.

Clover was still struggling with her sprained ankle, trying not to groan with pain. Eventually the man lost interest and entered his apartment, along with another man.

An alley was near the car. Duala ran to it (Clover hopped) and hoped that they could jump onto the roof of the apartment from the top of the alley. Duala heard a strange noise coming from the general direction of a ladder—a purring sound.

They crept along the alleyway onto the ladder. Duala climbed up to investigate. "Clover, we can go into their apartment from here!" Duala whisper-shouted. There was a loud and sudden crash.

"Hey, Duala, you think you can help me?" Clover's shirt was torn, exposing her lower belly and a little bit of her back. Her chest was scratched and her arm was bleeding. "I was about to climb up the ladder when this cat jumped on me out of nowhere. Then I fell against the ladder and it collapsed. I realized that the cat had torn out a part of my shirt. I didn't know that I'd bonked my head against the wall until the cat scratch pain eased a little."

"Clover, I left the medical kit in the bike basket. I'll go get it. Hopefully the cat won't injure both of us. Just wait here, okay?" Duala told Clover.

"Oh, be careful, Duala . . . all right, fine."

Duala went to the part of the outer brick wall and placed her foot on a foothold. Her other foot went to a higher foothold. She crouched down with her hands still up as far as they could go. She repeated the process going down, down, down. She thought she saw a tabby cat streaking down the sidewalk. Duala hadn't realized that she was so far down already. A litter of orange striped kittens were meowing in a garbage bag. "I wonder if they like milk," she said to herself. Duala laughed. "Of course they do!"

Then she remembered that she had milk in her medical kit left over from the plane's ride. She hurried down and grabbed the medical kit. Duala poured some milk into her cupped hand and lowered her palm. The hungry kittens licked it eagerly. She pet a couple of them, since Duala wasn't afraid of rabies, and, seeing a blur of a cat come back, she poured the leftover milk into the trash bag and hurried back up the ladder. For some reason, Duala always had the right thing at the right time.

Clover was waiting, bored. "I guess you've got it?" she asked. She pointed at the case Duala was holding. "Well, the cat's here for a good reason, if she's taking care of her litter."

Duala opened her small white kit and handed a strip of bandage to Clover. She closed her kit and watched as Clover wound the bandage over her scratches.

"How do you think we'll get inside? I mean, it's got windows. You have a hammer or something?" Clover joked. "The only way that's *not* certain to get us in jail is hoping the windows are unlocked. Want to try that?"

"Sure," Duala said. The two buildings were almost touching, so they had no risk of falling. Clover reached out and tried to pull the window to the side. It didn't work. "Wait, Clover . . . try to push it in. My fingernails are cut. You do it." Duala let Clover cautiously climb onto the woody window ledge. "Wait! Are they in there? We can't go in if they're still in there."

"Two men are in there. They didn't see me, though, and they just left. Maybe it's something important. I'll follow them wherever they're going, and you stay and observe. I'll . . . honk the bike's horn when they're coming back. Don't worry, it won't call attention to itself. There's a person doing it right now!" Clover said, laughing.

Before Clover managed to jump onto the ground, Duala put a hand on Clover's shoulder. "You'll be an elephant in a haystack. You'll stand out with scratches like that. Take my jacket." Duala took off her jacket and shivered in the slight breeze. Even the softest wind was, to her, ice-cold.

"Thanks," Clover said gratefully as she stuck her sticklike arms through the jacket. She zipped it up. "See you!" she called, swinging through the alleyway and dodging a cat's claw.

Duala then crawled through the window, aware that what she was doing was trespassing. It *was* against the law, but . . . did she have a choice? What was she supposed to do, wait for the two men to invite her in for tea?

She read three pages of writing in a journal that she'd found on a desk, and then used a fingerprint-saving device called a FingerTack to save the fingerprint of whoever owned the journal.

Hello Journal,

Jay has kidnapped me. I first saw him in a shop where he was picking out clothes. He saw my brother and I chatting over minerals and jewels, since Ronald has a degree in mining engineering. I am studying it. It was then that he came up to us and asked if we would like to own a gem store. I said yes, and my brother Ronald said maybe.

He followed us home without us knowing it and waited till dark to kidnap us. We were thrown into his black sedan and taken to a house in Durango.

He knocked us out with his knockout spray and drove us here, so that is all I remember.

When we are in the apartment, Jay keeps an eye on it so that we will not escape against his will. Neither Ronald nor I have worked up the courage to escape by the window. We both know that Jay keeps an eye on the window, or so he says.

Duala laughed. "Or so he says," she repeated. "Well, we proved that wrong." She continued reading.

Jay keeps the diamond in his apartment, but he forgot it here when he left. He is forgetful and once forgot his laptop when he was visiting. He came back for it, though. He should be coming

*back for the diamond in an hour. He remembers
things shortly after he forgets them.*

*Good-bye, ciao, au revoir, and so long,
Journal!*

Elliot

Meanwhile, Clover flipped on her sunglasses as she walked through the street, trailing the dust trail left by the car. The men had driven off and Clover couldn't see the car anymore, but she knew the license plate number, so as she walked, she checked the cars.

After only a few minutes of walking, Clover passed a salon with a red convertible beside it. The automobile also had the same license number as the car the girls had seen at the airport, so Clover entered the hair salon.

Duala rummaged through the closet as Clover walked into the salon. She searched through all the things. It seemed like a pretty clean closet. Duala even shook everything in there thrice before being sure the diamond wasn't hidden in the old-fashioned elm closet.

She never found it, even though she was in there for what seemed like forever to her, and she went through the objects at least three times. Then Duala straightened up and smacked her forehead with her palm. Jay must have already come for the diamond. Or maybe Elliot took it with him when he went out.

Either way, she was sure that the diamond was not hidden in this house.

She never had in mind that maybe the thieves were coming back until she heard Clover's horn. It was fancy, but it was noisy. She dropped everything and ran. Duala was a little slow, but she still got down in time. The car was nowhere in sight, but that was because only Elliot had entered the apartment and Ronald had driven away. Clover beckoned to Duala—she had found something. Duala ran down to Clover and was shocked by what she found.

A bystander would never notice, but if you inspected the sidewalk closely, you could see a fingerprint, and a red one—probably blood. Duala told Clover, "Diamonds are sharp. Maybe while this person was carrying it, it cut his or her fingers." She took out her exclusive FingerTack, pressed a sheet of special paper to the sidewalk on the fingerprint, and put it back inside her FingerTack. She always carried her FingerTack, scissors, and the first-aid kit with her—you'd never know exactly when you'd need to use them.

It was definitely Ronald's fingerprint—the fingernumber was the same as the one on the journal (fingertacks saved fingerprints with numbers). The girls saw their high-tech bike, now a golden ring, in the middle of the street, and they went to go get it.

Airborne, they scanned the streets for Ronald's car. Clover told Duala the story at the salon:

She was walking, and when she entered the salon, a man was holding something tightly in a fist of pinkish sweat. It was small. The exact size of Maple's Gem Shop's diamond.

So then she took her moneybag and found that she had $122.98 (with some of her parents' money, of course)—enough for an appointment at Jay's Hair Salonne for her, which was the name of the salon. Besides, Clover wanted her hair curled so badly that she would sacrifice all of her money for it.

The two went in, and Clover asked for her fiery bangs to be dyed blond and curled. The girl at the desk was a teenager. The teenage girl nodded and led Duala to a seat.

"My name's Clairi. Well, I expect you want my real name—It's Clairane." Clairi asked, "What school do you go to? I know all the schools in this district. You must be from somewhere far away if I don't know your school." Clover nodded, her temporarily red bangs shaking.

"I'm from Minnesota. Far, right?" she said with a sly smile. Of course, this wasn't true; it was only a lie, in case Clairi would use the real information. You could never tell. Clairi nodded, with her eyes open wide.

"What brings you here? Vacation?" Clairi asked.

"Yup. My aunt lives in New Jersey and she invited me there, so I'm staying in an apartment with my parents for now." Clover kept her voice light and casual.

Clover's hair was just completing its drying process (her hair had to be washed) when the man Clover had seen on the airplane walked out of the room with an "Employees Only" sign hanging on its door.

"Yes, we're going to Mexico soon—well, only Jay is. So I'll have to take over," the man told a strict-looking woman. He looked relieved, for some reason.

In the middle of Clover's story, Duala shook her head. "Clover! Wake up! How can we get to Mexico if we don't have any more money? How else can we get there?"

"Private jet?" Clover suggested.

"Oh! How come I never thought of that? That's *it,* Clover! You're a genius! We're going to Mexico all right, but not on a plane. Daddy will lend us his private jet!" Duala exclaimed, grinning.

Clover and Duala used the bike to ride to Clover's aunt Meg's café. She was just closing down the restaurant, she said, but they were welcome to stay. While the girls sat at a hickory table and drank Meg's delicious hot chocolate (Duala, who considered herself quite grown-up, sipped some coffee).

"Aunt Meg," Duala began. (She called Clover's dad Dad, her aunt Aunt Meg, and her grandfather Grandpa, since they were almost sisters.) Meg turned with a flash of her curly red hair and eyes green like jade.

"Mmm-hmm?" Meg asked.

"I was wondering, the day after tomorrow, can we . . . leave?" Duala inquired shyly.

"Of course. Leave when you want, or even stay forever," Meg said with a good-natured smile. She tossed her hair to the side.

"Good, because we're going to Mexico," Duala said, satisfied.

CHAPTER 2

The jet ride was chaos. They encountered a storm where Clover tipped from side to side, but Duala just sat on a white leather couch, sipping apple juice slowly.

The room was in an oval shape. In the center of the room was a steel table with a glass top. To the left of the table, if you were standing at the juniper door, there was a white leather couch. It was six feet long, the same length as the table. To the right of the table, there were three white leather chairs. A gray leather recliner almost blocked your view of the table, if you were standing at the door.

Next to the doorway was a long, curved black couch, and it was made of leather. It was about fifteen feet long, but since it was curved, it looked a little shorter. One antelope skin pillow was propped up on the couch's left armrest, and against the right armrest was a zebra skin pillow.

There was a 72-inch plasma TV on the wall next to the door, and on the other side of the room was a duplicate of that television, so one could watch television without having another person's head blocking the view.

There was a round desk taking up some empty space. There was no place to charge electronic devices, but this was the ideal place you sat when you wanted to turn on your laptop, unless, of course, you would rather lie down on a couch to type. It was more commonly used as a dining table, though sometimes one ate on the couch.

The carpet under the table was zebra skin, but the rest of the carpet was leopard skin. Duala did not especially like this, since she was an animal lover, but Clover had thrown many of what Duala called "hissy fits" because of the carpeting.

There were windows on the sides of the room, and the French doors, made out of juniper but painted a creamy white, led to the bedroom.

The bedroom was a smaller room than the one with the two TV's. On one side of the oval room was a fluffy bed, and on the other side was a smaller fluffy bed. The bigger one was for "guests," Duala's dad said, but he actually meant friends. The smaller bed was for frequent fliers. Duala was classified as a frequent flier, so the bigger bed was for Clover. Duala's dad had a special bed all to himself, as he was the pilot.

Duala and Clover went to sleep quickly. Duala's dream was totally crazy—a diamond was chasing her—but the next day, she could remember nothing about it. The jet would arrive at the nearest airport, where the girls would hopefully see the thieves again. Well, now that Duala had read the diary entry, she knew that it was a *thief,* not *thieves.*

It was almost late afternoon when Duala finally woke up, but now that she had, it was like she had just swallowed ten sodas. "Clover! There's Mexico!" Duala yelled. Clover woke up grumpily and grunted something that sounded a bit like "Gerrumph."

Clover repeated the sound. "Gerrumph! Gerrumph—*aah!*" She shook her leg and a ball of wet fur flew up. Duala cracked up.

"Looks like Daddy performed his wet-fur-ball prank again. He always does that," Duala explained with a smirk. "Get up. We're almost there."

When they got near Mexico, Duala's first task was to try and spot the thief. She did not spot any of them. Duala knew that the airport would not give out any information regarding its passengers, so it would be useless to ask the airport staff about an Elliot, Ronald, or Jay. Besides, the girls didn't even know their last names. As the jet got closer, Duala watched the passengers intently, but still could not see the men.

Her dad, Hugo March, landed the jet on a space reserved for him. All the passengers had boarded the plane. The girls, with Duala's dad, walked to the nearest street and got a taxi to stop. Then they rode to a hotel.

The hotel wasn't a luxury, but it was close enough. Duala's only complaint was that there was no flower next to the bathtub. Clover had rolled her eyes when she'd heard this. Clover had never been to a hotel with a flower next to the bathtub. *And this*, she thought, *was heaven*.

The next day, Clover woke up earlier than the rest of them. She brushed her teeth and ate an apple as her breakfast. Then she washed her face and took a shower, and when she got out Duala was still snoring—*on the floor*. Clover had to pinch herself to keep from laughing. Duala had rolled from the bed onto the floor, and she was still sleeping. Duala was a huge sleeper, which was pretty unusual, since she was very organized—the more organized of the girls.

Just as Clover crept up to scare Duala into wakefulness, Duala jumped. She looked around. "How did I get on the floor?" she asked, confused.

"Um, you rolled yourself off the bed," Clover replied.

"Without waking up?" Duala asked.

"Without waking up," Clover agreed.

"Daddy! What's the nearest airport in Mexico to New York?" Duala called. Her dad was asleep in another room.

The reply was received instantly. "Piedros Nagras Airport. Want to go there?"

Duala shouted, "Yes! Of course!" back to her dad, then turned to Clover. "Now, where to stay?" Duala asked, and then bit her lower lip.

"Ick," Clover said under her breath. Duala's lips were smothered with lipstick. Duala never wiped her lipstick off, except for when she ate and at really crazy parties.

Somehow, though, Duala managed to bite her lip without getting any mushy red stuff on it.

Duala made a monster face at Clover and bit her lip again, without getting any lipstick on her teeth. Clover pretended to gag. "How do you wear that stuff?" Clover asked, disgusted. It wasn't the first time.

Duala batted her eyelashes. "I have my secrets," she said, smirking.

Duala's dad reserved a space at the airport to land, and once he did, they were off. Duala snoozed ("Catching up on my sleep that *you* disturbed," she'd said to Clover) off in the bedroom while Clover messed around on Duala's laptop, finally resetting the screensaver, much to Duala's exasperation. ("If you want to mess around on a laptop, go get your own," she'd said.)

This time, the girls spotted the men, and an unfamiliar man between the two. "That must be Jay," Clover whispered. Duala nodded quietly.

The man in the middle did not have Elliot's red hair or Ronald's beard. Instead, he had a tie and a top hat, and Duala thought he looked almost like a magician. *Nobody would think of him being a thief,* Duala thought.

Jay gave Elliot a little slip of money and Elliot walked with Jay to the entrance of the airport, where Elliot slipped Jay the diamond in its pouch. Duala could hardly see the movement. It was very swift and quick.

A few minutes later both men walked out of the door, where Ronald was waiting. Ronald jerked his head toward Jay's car and the trio walked toward the car.

Jay entered his car and closed the door. Naturally Elliot and Ronald followed after him, but the man didn't give them an invitation into his car. He just got in and started driving. Elliot ran, yelling things so muffled the girls could not understand, after the car. Ronald sat back onto a fence post and waited for Elliot to come back.

The girls said good-bye to Duala's dad quickly. They were both going to visit Duala's Uncle Carlos, who lived in Piedros Nagras. Duala grabbed her ring and turned it into a bike just in time to see Jay drive out of the parking lot.

Pretty soon both girls were up in the air, Clover pedaling as fast as she could, eager to get to Jay as quick as possible, and Duala pedaling softly, taking her time. Duala, who was in front and could control the bike, shot down to the ground and rode all the way to the river, where she rode with the current. Jay had headed in the direction the river was going, which was north. She applied waterwheels and oars.

They followed the fiery red car as long as they could. Duala's legs began to ache. The bike would not run out of energy, as it was solar-powered and saved 50 percent of the energy made for the night. The other 50 percent went into the moment.

She stopped outside of a big, army-green building made of bricks.

CHAPTER 3

The girls crept up against the smooth building and peeked in a window. Jay and another man were talking casually. The door was firmly closed and newly painted green. Duala made a mental list of all the details. She was picky about doors and had actually moved in to Clover's house once just because the paint on her door was chipped and Duala didn't want to be embarrassed by her door.

Clover snatched the earscope from her baggy pocket and put it on her ear.

"Now, how about we talk about the diamond? Could I please have your offer?" Jay asked.

"Well, I'll give it to you if you give me your diamond."

"How about we exchange the items at the same time?" Jay asked.

"Um, okay," said the other man.

"What will you give me for the diamond?"

"A million."

"What! Well, the deal's on." Jay looked flabbergasted at the other man's offer. The diamond was small; he probably thought it was only worth about ten thousand dollars.

The girls burst out laughing hard.

"What's that noise?" Jay yelled. The girls stayed against the wall, motionless. They didn't know that Jay was coming for them. One more step and he would reach them . . .

But no. As he reached out for the door handle, the diamond scattered out of his pocket almost as if it was waiting for just the right moment. As he looked down, Clover looked in the window, turned her head, and nodded, mouthing, "Get in!" Just when Jay was about to kneel down and grab the diamond, Duala knew it was time to open the door.

The beginner spy threw open the door with such force that it knocked Jay out cold. The doorknob had hit him in his stomach and his forehead while he was kneeling down.

Duala kneeled down to pick the diamond up. The other man, previously motionless, ran to get it, but Clover was too quick for him. She snatched the diamond from Duala and threw it into her pocket. The other man looked up at Duala coldly and walked back into the building. He picked up a gem.

"Are you good at races?" he asked. A smile formed on his lips. "If you can win a race with me and my motorcycle, you get this gem and keep the diamond, but if you do not win, you give the diamond. Beware—my motorcycle's high-tech. Very high-tech."

"I accept," said Duala bravely under his stare. "As long as your motorcycle isn't solar power."

"Blah. My motorcycle is electronic."

They raced for three hours. Duala had the sun on her side. She, of course, went into high-flying position. Duala punched a button in her bike that made it speed up even more than with the glider—the bike now had a helicopter fan! The little fan was stuck to the bottom and on the back was a big one. Of course, the wheels formed into the fans. She was way ahead of the man—almost half a mile ahead! She could see him, too, and he was flying.

He was speeding up.

Suddenly he made a sharp turn; Duala followed. He was heading for the river. Duala lowered herself and realized that he slowed down when he was a half-mile away from the river.

She lost all transformations of her bike, so that now it was a normal bike, and freefell into the river. Then she made her bike swim ahead of his motorcycle. The sun was still bright. It was still hard work, but Duala pedaled as hard as she could. She realized that he was slowing down fast. She hopped up onto the bank of the river. Duala waited for him. Once he slowed to a stop, she held her hand out.

"Gem, please?"

The man smirked. "Never!" he sneered.

"I guess not," Duala said, then made a dive for his pocket. Caught off guard, the man tumbled to the ground. For a second, Duala thought that this would be like stealing, but then she thought, *he should be fair when he's made a bet and lost it.*

Duala dug her hand into his left pocket and triumphantly pulled out a pink jewel. She did not gloat over her success. The man would soon be on his feet again. She sped back to Clover, who was almost asleep.

A week later, Duala was home in Pagosa again. She turned a pink Valentine from school over and over in her hands. Returning the crystal clear gem to Maple's Gemstore would be a challenge—the gem shop was miles away in Denver, Colorado. So then, a week later, she traveled again. And returning the pinkish-red gem to the other store, well, that would be even more.

Duala walked down the streets of the snowy Canyon Drive. She thought about where the pink gem might've come from. "Maybe I should check the Internet for recent robberies in America. Or maybe I should contact my long-distance friends and tell them to read up on newspaper articles. I will do both. I will get more accurate results that way," the young girl said to herself.

She searched on Google, Yahoo, and other countless search engines "recent robberies in America." There was one article about Sandy 'Quariums Gift Shop, but she overlooked it, as no word sprang out at her as she read a part of it.

However, she did get some news from her friends. One of them lived near Long Beach, California, and said that a gift shop with a jewelry section in it had had their fifth steal of the month!

One day, she went to return the diamond to Maple's Gem Shop. Maple seemed surprised that Duala was there. Duala put a huge grin on her face and announced that she had the diamond. She placed it on the glass counter. Maple looked at it, and her face burst into a big smile.

"Finally! I'd been searching for you all over, Duala. We've closed down, so I was surprised that someone just walked in *rudely like you did!*" Maple joked.

"Well, of course, I had to grow more impolite, with all those centuries away from civilization!" Duala told Maple. Maple and Duala had been buddies in school. When Duala was a homeschooled kindergartner, Maple was in eighth grade, babysitting Duala. Now Maple had just got out of a college near town.

"Anyway, thanks a million for the diamond. I knew you'd get it. I will pay you ten thousand dollars now, as it said on the sign I posted," Maple said. Duala shook her head no and was walking out the door when she turned around suddenly and asked a question.

"You wouldn't happen to know a quick way to get to Southern California, would you? Daddy's at the doctor, really sick with the flu, so he can't fly us there."

Maple said, "Tell you what, I can give you the money for airplane tickets and other expenses you need to cover.

Ten thousand dollars should cover it. I'll give you the cash."

"Thank you so much, Maple! You're the best!" Duala exclaimed as she collected the money and ran out the door.

CHAPTER 4

The next day, a flight came. The four-hour flight departed with the two girl spies on it. Two naps later, the girls woke up to find that they had almost arrived at the airport.

The two split up after they biked to where they could see the ocean and each walked a different direction. They'd agreed to get back together by the ocean. Duala had, in her head, an image of the compass, and she started facing the ocean. She knew that way was west, so she knew which way was north, south, east, or west. But finally she quit using that strategy and just head in the direction of the ocean. She came to lots of shops with gems in them, but none of them were in Long Beach.

Then, finally, after miles of walking, Duala came to a small beach with aquariums on the shore. She quickly skimmed over all the stores, but found none with gems in them. Then she found a boy a little taller than her next to the beach. He was counting jewels. Jewels! Duala walked up next to him and asked, "Are you missing a pink gem?"

"Pftt! No pink gems for me . . . I only get red, blue, green, et cetera gems in my—my collection. But not pink! Pink's a girl color, and besides, almost nobody has pink," the boy said. He didn't realize that he had given away a clue.

He could be a thief. I'd better go somewhere else. Don't want him stealing all the gems, do I? thought Duala.

The boy put his gems into a napkin, and he stood up and walked away. Duala watched the store he went into. It was a gift shop with a jewel section!

CHAPTER 5

*D*uala followed the boy into the store, then saw that the tanks up next to the window held oodles of gems. She went right up to the main desk, and asked, "Do you have a pink-red gem stolen?"

"Yes, it is in the shape of a slight heart. Do you have it?" the woman asked. Duala took the beautiful, shimmering jewel out, looked at it closely, and discovered that it *was* in the shape of a heart—there was a slight crease on the opposite side of the sharp point.

"Yeah, here it is," Duala said. She smiled, and handed the gem to the woman.

"Oh, my . . . thank you so much! I have a favor to ask of you. Now, you've retrieved this gem, and we have quite a couple of gems missing. So, I don't mean to get you too busy, in case you're tracking down some other priceless jewels . . . but you know, almost half of our gems are missing now. All in two months. So, it's okay

if you say no, but would you track down some of them?"
the woman asked.

"I'd be glad to!" Duala said. The woman smiled.

The next day, Duala received a message on her cell
phone from her dad: he had gotten better from the flu,
good enough to fly Duala back to Pagosa. So since she
had to get home somehow, she texted her dad that he
should pick her up at 6:30 p.m. on the next day. She had
received the message on Saturday, so her dad had plenty
of time to fly here and back.

Clover and Duala met by the ocean that night and
rode their bike to a comfortable enough spot to settle.
That night they traded watch shifts, and Clover took
the first watch while Duala settled down with a thin
body heat-reflecting sleeping bag in the bike's secret
compartment.

On the jet, Duala searched the Internet for Sandy
'Quariums, the name of the gift shop she had visited. She
found a whole page on the history of Sandy 'Quariums:

> *Sandy 'Quariums aquarium and jewel shop
> has suffered, but lived through, a series of gem
> thievery. Suspects and neighbors have been
> interviewed, but none of them seem to be the
> thief. Some have provided interesting and valued
> information, though.*
>
> *Mason Nosum: "I used to work at Sandy
> 'Quariums as a teenager, and there were some
> major gem crimes happening. I lived through
> it. One day, I was walking home from school,*

starting to enter the shop, when I saw a teenage boy counting gems! He finished counting the gems and entered the shop. That was forty years ago;I think he was the thief. He probably has a son or daughter now who steals just like him now! So I say, somebody better catch that thief!"

Carrie Ingle: "I live next to Sandy 'Quariums, and I have a report of, supposedly, a crime of gems: I was up late one night and looking out the window when I saw a dark shape in the night by the ocean. The shape seemed to be that of a human, and he or she was counting things. The things sparkled in the dark just like gems would; the next day, there was a report of a stolen gem. I hope that we catch the thief, whatever we need to do. I thought the human figure was a child, or at the very oldest a teenager. Hopefully no more kids will go mad with thievery!"

There was more to it, but Duala was, by then, too tired to read more; Duala had walked almost a mile to get to the jet because the ring was with Clover.

When Duala got to Pagosa, she saw Clover strolling down Blockway Street. Duala ran to Clover and told her what she had discovered about the stolen jewels from Sandy 'Quariums. Clover nodded and asked Duala, "Hey, can we have a sleepover tonight? Well, actually, for the whole week . . . My parents are out of town, and they asked me to go to your house for the period of time they're gone. So, anyway, can I?"

"Sure!"

"Cool. Anyway, wait a couple minutes for me; I have to get my stuff."

While Clover was gone, Duala hurriedly threw the pillows over the floor, put up mirrors all over the walls, turned off the lights, and lit three tiny LEDs in the middle of the floor.

Duala attached a homemade switch to the circuit. She tested it. When the circuit was closed, the room was filled with light, and when it was open, the room was pitch-black. The light bulbs were different-colored. They were red, blue, and yellow: the three primary colors. The room was a rainbow with the light bulbs. If Duala was little, she would be searching for a pot of gold right now, but now Duala didn't believe in pots of gold.

Duala put some pieces of carpet with holes in them over the circuit. The light shone through the centimeter-wide, inch-long holes, making ovals of light on the walls.

Clover arrived just as Duala put new flowers in the flower vase. The lights were off and streamers had been put up so that they hung over every doorway and wall you could see, not including the mirrors, of course.

"Woah! This is supercool, Duala, but don't you think we're missing a sound system?" Clover asked. "Or do I just not see it because the lights are off?"

"Oh, you're never seeing it in this sleepover!" Duala said. She felt her way to the sound system, which was hidden under a table behind streamers. "Let the slumber party begin!"

Duala turned around and felt along the floor to the switch for the light bulbs. She turned them on.

"Totally cool!" Clover shouted. She was dancing to a song.

"Hey, what do you want to do? Let's not work on the case this sleepover—let's just have fun, 'kay?" Duala asked. "Hopefully can find some clues . . . but anyway, for now, we'll go to the park. Okay?"

"Sure! Hey, let's go to that doggie hotel and pick up Jackie. Then we can walk her and play with her in the park," Clover said. Jackie was the almost magically bouncy Chihuahua with gigantically cute ears and an adorable stare.

Duala walked to the doggie hotel, Paws and Playtime, to pick up her Chihuahua with Clover at her side. The miniature puppy, black all over except for her golden eyebrows, white cross on her chest, and red stripe down her nose, sprang up. She immediately started barking and howling at the sight of Duala. Jackie could eat like a vacuum cleaner! She was shipped to Duala from Norway, but though Duala often kept her up until 8:00 p.m. (and that was 10:00 p.m. in Norway), she never ran out of energy.

When Jackie's ginormous cage was open, she dashed out just like a flame when a match is struck. Jackie ran around in circles, nearly tripping over her paws in an attempt to speed up; Jackie's head was launched forward, while her rear paws were parallel to her neck, in front of her front paws. Her front paws were pulled backward, and as she ran, she toppled forward on her front paws. In midair, her paws were all spread out, like she was trying to hide something invisible.

Duala led Jackie out and into the park. Jackie sniffed the air, barked, and started toward Duala's back jean pocket. Jackie thrust her head in, grabbing the treat Duala had put in. She giggled—Jackie tickled!

Duala and Clover trained her dog, groomed her, and fed her, of course. By the time they were beginning to get hungry, it was already dark. The girls ran home with Jackie in Duala's bag, ate some chips, and went to bed.

The whole week, Clover and Duala were having fun.

Then, after the week was over, they flew to Long Beach—again. Clover and Duala camped out, roasting marsh-mellows and wading out into the salty waters. They had water fights all day, but at night, they kept an eye out for the boy. Duala and Clover only took marshmallows and a blanket with them, so they wouldn't be easily spotted in the wrap of black night.

Even though they had fun at daytime, nighttime was a period of perilous waiting. After three solid nights of waiting, they saw him.

Duala and Clover were having a water fight when they heard footsteps. Like they always did when they heard footsteps, Duala picked up the marsh-mellows and Clover wrapped up the blanket, and they ducked down behind a picnic table. What he took out of his pocket shocked both Clover and Duala—a legendary crystal bar! There were only about fifty left in the world, or so it was rumored.

The perfectly clear bar of diamond had sprinkles of crystal in it, a rare happening. Sometimes, a diamond somehow met the crystal, but the sharp, piercing diamond would sometimes crush the delicate crystal, and the crystal would stick to the diamond. It rarely happened, but it happened.

Obviously the crystal bar needed to become a *bar*. People say there were crystal bars all around us in the time of the dinosaurs. But then a giant meteorite fell and destroyed most of the crystal bars. The few that were left were in pieces. But the day mining started, they found how to make crystal bars again.

You take a diamond and a crystal, smashing them together. The sharpness of the diamond will shatter the delicate crystal structure, leaving miniature crystal specks on the diamond. Then the diamond is run in hot water and placed in the snow for an exact day. If the moment it was placed in the snow was at 6:32 one day, the next day it should be picked out of the snow at 6:32. After it dries, it will become sort of a bar shape. Crystal bars are not made with machines, so they aren't perfect bars. They are only long lumps of crystal and diamond—but they *are* rare, and extremely valuable.

The boy pulled the perfectly clear crystal bar out of his pocket, put it back in, and looked around. Clover and Duala stayed perfectly hidden behind the wooden, blanket-covered picnic table. The boy dug a hole in the sand, still looking around. He buried it and entered Sandy 'Quariums. While he was gone, Duala ran to the bunch of sand and dug. Clover helped her.

Pretty soon, they had the crystal bar in their hands. Duala shoved it under the picnic table and whisper-shouted to Clover, "Clover! Pretend we just got here, and don't even *look* at the picnic table. 'Kay?"

The girls left their blanket under the picnic table as well, but they ate their marshmallows, lying in the water. When the boy came out, he started to dig into the hole Clover had filled up again, but when he saw the girls, he stopped. He casually walked away from the hole and took some sand to sprinkle around it. He pretended he was building . . . a fence? Yes, most likely a fence.

"Come on, Clover. We can wrap it up in the blanket," Duala whispered into Clover's ear.

So the girls wrapped the gem up in the blanket, ignoring a curious look from the culprit. As they entered the store, they took the gem out from the blanket. The woman at the counter exclaimed, "Yes! You found my most prized gem! Now, who's the culprit?"

"Him," Duala said, throwing her thumb over her shoulder so that it pointed at the boy.

CHAPTER 6

*D*uala woke up early one morning and got herself some cereal. She called Clover and told her to meet Duala at the park. Ten minutes later, they met.

"Clover, I think someone—or rather, a group of someones—is behind all this. Are they making those thieves steal things? It's just not normal for all these gem things to happen at the same time! I think we should look into Elliot's diary *one* more time . . . ," Duala told Clover.

"Good thinking, but we should probably wait. There's been a lot of traveling for the past month, and my dad is getting exasperated at the amount of traveling I'm doing," Clover said, her voice hard. Duala knew she was lying. Clover's dad had a job, and even though he loved Clover a lot, he would probably be freed of a small burden if Clover went away—not forever, of course, since he would be like the living dead then, but for a short time.

Clover was still scared of airplanes. Duala could tell by the nervousness in Clover's voice, and her own voice was bitter as she said her own regretful words.

"Oh, and I suppose your *mom* wouldn't approve," Duala shot back. She was getting tired of this stupid fear. Seriously, when would a plane really crash? And even if it did, would she and Clover really *die?*

Clover turned her face a mask of anger. "My mom would approve very much, and you know that. Your mom would, too, and you know *that,* too." Her words hit Duala in the chest like arrows, and Duala was slapped by how very *stupid* she'd been. Duala had backed down from a fight more than once, and this was one of those times. But before she had a chance to apologize, Clover turned on her heel and stomped away.

Which left Duala with her own feelings.

One week passed. Two weeks. Three weeks after the conflict, Duala walked to the park and met Clover, who wasn't sobbing. Well, that was no surprise. Clover never sobbed, and Duala had only seen a tear cross Clover's face once, when Clover had broken her arm. Not when Clover had broken her thumb, or taken around ten IV shots because of a huge gash in her forehead, or when she had gotten the gash.

Duala was surprised to see Clover catch a frog in the park pond. Clover had no love for frogs, Duala knew. Or thought. And Clover was . . . *stroking* it on the top of its head! And talking to it! *Well,* thought Duala, *maybe we aren't non-identical twins who were attached at the hip and separated at birth.* This girl was certainly a new girl.

The new girl did something just like the old girl. She lifted her nose in the air, and turned her face to Duala's. "Hi, person I don't know," the new-and-old girl called. "Come see Tickle."

Duala scrunched up her face in disgust. A frog was enough. Stroking a frog and talking to it was more than enough. But naming it, of all things, *Tickle?* That was a dog name, not a frog name. Duala felt ready to scold Clover again. Maybe yell at her.

But her bubble had not been completely punctured yet. Actually, not at all—*she* was the one who had done the puncturing. Clover's bubble—actually, Clover liked to call it a balloon—had not burst yet. Bubbles often burst with a *pop.* Balloons, if you burst them correctly, could burst with a *scissssshhhhhh.*

It would seem like the other way around, but Clover was the balloon and Duala was the bubble. Clover, right now, seemed as if she was bursting with a *scissssshhhhhh.* She smiled a crooked smile and made an effort to skip away, but it looked more like she was a giraffe who tried to swim with jelly legs. Duala stifled a laugh. Clover had never quite mastered the art of skipping.

Duala wasn't going to let the swimming giraffe with jelly legs get away. "Hey! Clo-ver! Stop!" Duala shouted. She walked a few paces forward and cupped her hands around her mouth. "Kuh-*loh*-ver! You—you forgot something!"

Clover apparently believed that she'd forgotten something, since she forgot things a lot, and she threw

Tickle up in the air. "No! Tickle! I forgot something!" she said as she caught her frog.

Duala did her best not to smile, but she could feel the corners of her mouth inching upwards. "Um, you forgot—your—green pencil!" Duala finished, producing a stray green pencil she had in her pocket.

"I . . . did? I didn't know I had a green pencil! Thank you, person I don't know," Clover said, evidently struggling with the prospect of not saying Duala's name. Duala took a deep breath and continued.

"I wanted to say—um—sorry? Sorry, I guess," Duala said quickly, in case Clover turned into a swimming giraffe with jelly legs again. Clover frowned.

"Well, if that's all you were going to tell me, I'll be off. Meet me at my house tomorrow evening at seven," Clover said cheerfully, and quickly turned into a swimming giraffe with jelly legs again.

Duala translated that into "I forgive you" in her head.

The next week, the girls set off again. They used the GPS on the bike to track down the apartment, since Duala remembered that it was somewhere near Second Street.

The apartment was empty—Duala's Humanitor, which could tell you if there were people in a ten-yard radius, told her that—so the girls crept inside, looking for the diary in a messy drawer. The diary was found under a pile of salt. Duala started searching for the most recent entry.

Hello Journal,

Jay has just told me that to receive my family, I must visit Victor Hickory. The headquarters is close to Jay's hair salon. The place there looks like an old shed, but it's actually an underground headquarters. He controls all the gem thievery groups.

Good-bye, Journal.

Duala and Clover decided what they should do: put on their camouflage suits and creep into the shed. *How hard it must've been to break into places in the old days*, Duala thought. They didn't even believe in this kind of stuff, did they?

They put on their suits and peeked inside the shed. There was wood walls, so the girls pressed the "wood" buttons on their suits and the one-piece metal suits instantly changed so that it looked like wood.

As they crept through one of the holes made by the broken planks of wood, Clover noted that a robot was rolling around on its side. Both sides had wheels, and it was dusting glass cases—cases of gems, Clover realized!

As they crept through the shed, they went lower and lower through a set of shining, marble stairs. Suddenly, a robot appeared, its head swiveling from side to side, its laser eyes going up and down so fast, it was all just a blur. When the lasers reached the girls, they froze. The robot's head convulsed, leaving an alarm in its place. The alarm beeped furiously, shooting sheets of sticky fabric all over the place. They hit Duala and Clover so fast that the girls were soon covered in sticky stuff.

Then the floor dropped . . . something was happening . . . a bare room appeared . . . it was gone . . . then a prisoner's room appeared . . . it was gone again . . . and finally, they hit the bottom of a cage. The robot bowed, and then its head twirled around and around so fast, and with so much force that the robot flew up into the air.

The young detectives looked around. Young faces were on bodies, but clearly the bodies were not theirs. "Victor Hickory" or whoever he was had placed a chip in their brains. Duala had read about it, but it was only done either for power over others' minds or the power of reading each other's minds, if two got "twin chips" that could communicate by thought if one person sent a thought to the other.

Each "chipped" human raised its arms and the girls were so shocked they jumped—the arms were perfect silver! Knowing that they'd meet this fate soon, they both ran away as far as they could, but when they reached a dead end, they knew that they would need to fight.

Clover was being tackled by one of them, and Duala recognized that one—Clairi! Clover seemed to know it too. "Cla-airi—It's me, Clover!" Clover rasped through the firm grasp of Clairi. Clairi seemed to recognize Clover, but the chip in her brain wouldn't let her let go.

Clover finally summoned up the strength to give Clairi a weak kick in the stomach with all the strength she had. Though it was very weak, it worked. Clairi fell backwards, allowing Clover to regain her strength and start battling with Duala. Clairi, meanwhile, was unconscious. In her chipped state, she had never been unconscious before, or hurt at all—her reflexes were too fast for that, and her arms were hard—and she wouldn't get used to it. Ever.

CHAPTER 7

The next day, their arms turned to silver. The girls would sit all day long, a microscopic part of their brains churning and churning, thinking of how to escape, but a ginormous part of their brains was just resting. Sitting there. Not doing anything at all, except for telling the heart to breathe.

The girls sat there all day, all night, and sometimes, suddenly the part that was left of true Clover and true Duala came to life. The girls would bend the iron bars until they were broken, but the bars were so stable and strong that it would take days to bend the bar even an inch.

Then, suddenly, one day a bar fell near the area of Duala's chip. A flailing arm in Duala's sleep had knocked it off. Duala was her true self again. She woke up and tried to dent Clover's brain too, but Duala could barely carry her own arms, as they were still silver. Maybe the chip cut the nerves there or something. Besides, her head *hurt.* It was bleeding, but Duala was sure she did not have a concussion.

Then, she came up with an idea. Duala took ahold of Clover's arm and banged it against a partly bent iron bar with all her might. It fell, and Clover woke up. She was alive, yes, but was she herself?

"Clover. Are you chipped?" Duala whispered into Clover's ear. If Clover said no, Duala would never forgive herself for being so stupid.

"Maybe. What I might have achieved in the future if you hadn't given me a dent in my brain, I can only imagine. Anyway, let's get out of here!" Clover whispered loudly.

"We have a space. See if you can squeeze through."

They were skinny enough to squeeze through, but which way was which? How could they get out? The only way to get out was the spiral staircase, but Duala had a feeling that it wasn't the same one that the girls had crossed themselves.

Instead, they searched for some crack that they could pry open.

Duala found a small mouse hole, but it was too sturdy to break. Clover kept on tapping on the walls to test and see if they were hollow. She moved all around the walls, listening for something hollow, and after what felt like an hour of searching, she found a hollow wall!

Clover squeezed back into the cage and took Clairi's body out of it. She slammed Clairi's arm into the wall and the wall grew a small hole with cracks sprouting from it!

Duala heard the noise, and she hurried to pry open the hole. Clover stuck Clairi's arm inside and pulled, causing the cracks to fling apart and making a bigger hole. The hole was now big enough for Duala and Clover to crawl through. And so they did.

As soon as they crawled through, Clover and Duala fell. They fell for a long time, and then hit a bright, tiled floor. A loud gasp went up from a crowd—they were in what looked like an office.

Ugh. My head is bleeding and my butt is sore, and now I'll have to fight, thought Duala. She took her headband and wrapped it around her head wound. That would slow the bleeding. Though the flow of blood had ceased, Duala still felt like she was about to faint, and faint she did. Duala slumped down into an unconscious heap.

Clover almost groaned, but she knew Duala was very susceptible to blood loss and instead made her expression fiercer. She took her socks and pressed them against her forehead, where blood was spurting out unevenly.

"Those nosy, good-for-nothing spies . . . they're *girls!*" a man exclaimed.

"Hush, now, I'm a woman and you have me here! Get the ropes and the potion!" a young woman said.

So the man went into a dim-lit room, several minutes later returning with an armful of rope and a small bottle of something that smelled like wine. Clover felt like she was stuck to the floor.

The "crowd" was actually only three people—a good batch to fight off too, it looked like. The people were so skinny that they could fit inside Clover. But Clover let them talk. She could barely hear some of their quietly whispering voices: "Should we tie them up first, or give them the potion first?" "Potion!" "Rope!"

It was probably decided that the man would tie up the girls. He tied the girls' arms to their bodies. He didn't have enough rope to tie their legs up. Clover was silent. Then she had an idea. "Well, we won't escape now, so why not tell us what we've failed to accomplish?"

"No. You've made it far enough. You might make it farther. But I *will* tell you that I'm not your common villain. Oh no, I'm not that guy that steals jewels for fun." Here the man gestured to the other room. Clover didn't know it, but she could easily guess what was there. Jewels.

"No, I didn't even steal all these for trade or money. I have enough money as it is," the man admitted. "I stole them for the *power.* All these gems you've found? They give power to whoever holds them. Have you ever held a gem, and then a day after you let go of it, your luck turns around? You feel as if your life has no meaning? That's it. That's the secret. The whole purpose of this."

Now that the speech was done, Clover sprang up to fight the people. She kicked as hard as she tumbled into broad feet headfirst, and she even bit at the people's hands and arms. One time, Clover even tried to bite a man's arm, but he ducked, and she ended up biting his ear!

Duala then woke up and groggily stood. As soon as she took in the battle, she was up and kicking in no time.

Duala got a bite at the woman's nose too—it was the same situation as Clover's, only the woman turned her head sideways when ducking! The woman happened to be very prone to nosebleeds, and she bled out of the room.

Of course, the enemies fought too, mostly to defend themselves. They couldn't punch the girls' stomachs because it was wrapped up in rope, but they could bruise the girls' legs. Duala kept on letting Clover do her business with one man by pulling his arm down with her teeth (or trying to, anyway), while Duala snuck up on the person from behind and kicked him in the legs so that the man fell to the floor.

Leaving Duala to do the fighting, with the woman still having a major nosebleed, Clover left a message for the police station on her phone. Then she continued fighting again.

Clover got the woman some tissues (even *she* hated to see blood all over the place), Duala tripped people, and everything went on, until Clover finally remembered what they were fighting for and took the potion in her mouth. She threw it to the floor, where it shattered into a million pieces and spilled all poison. The men stared at the spiral of glass—they had been fighting Duala until they heard the clatter of shreds of ice.

"We totally forgot!" a man exclaimed, while the other man just mumbled an angry phrase to himself under his breath. They both searched for a weapon in a drawer, and they found one—a knife. Realizing that she and Clover could both be free with the help of that weapon, Duala kicked the man in the shin.

The man collapsed onto his knees, squeezing his eyes shut and swearing under his breath. Clover grabbed the knife with her hands and started loosening Duala's ropes. The other man was prodding the man with his shoe, muttering, "Get up! Get up!"

When a little more than half of Duala's ropes were cut, she wriggled through the ropes. Duala then started cutting through Clover's ropes when the police burst in!

"Great! You're finally here!" Clover exclaimed in surprise.

"Yes, and we're . . . What is this mess?" a male asked, clearly disgusted by the yellowish liquid flowing through the tiles, like cars moving through a highway.

"Oh, that's just poison. Nothing dangerous now," Duala replied. The men stared, dumbfounded, at the police who had just entered.

"Freeze," a strict-looking woman commanded. The thieves held up their hands, even the woman with the nosebleed. The woman inspected each thief and, after removing a firearm and a knife from the men, announced that they were now weapon-free. The policemen handcuffed the male thieves first, and then handcuffed the woman, whose nosebleed had stopped.

As the woman cut through the ropes surrounding the entwined Duala, she talked quietly. "You know, this is my first case. I've only been a policewoman for about a month. Oh, and you know, you've been a great help to all these gem shops—you've given them a strategy to track down little boys!" the policewoman chuckled.

CHAPTER 8

After being asked if they'd like to be escorted home, and permitting it, Duala and Clover walked up to a plane to go home.

Once the girls got there, Pagosa felt friendly and familiar. The girls were up in Duala's dad's helicopter taking a tour of the Rocky Mountains (Duala had taken this tour before, but Clover insisted on going, so Duala had to go with her.).

On the way back to Duala's house, the girls saw a hill covered with trees, but under the trees was a house. They could tell it was made of bricks. At that moment, Duala had an idea. A few years ago, her dad had purchased a large brick house on a hill. The family had never used it, but Duala thought of a way the house could be transformed into a home.

That day, they decided to establish a spy agency.

The spy agency was called Mountain Palace Spies, named after their house. The house was the headquarters. It looked fairly small, but there were around five underground chambers, each fairly large. The girls could easily imagine fitting a few blacksmith spies (amateur spies) into those chambers. Once the Head of Spies, the head of all spy agencies, approved Mountain Palace Spies, the agency would have some silversmiths (medium-level spies) and maybe even a couple of goldsmiths (professional spies). Duala and Clover were called jewelsmiths, the leaders of the agency.

In order for the Head of Spies to validate their agency, Duala and Clover would have to send a letter to them informing them that their agency was real. Later on, Duala did this with her neatest handwriting.

Dear Head of Spies,

Mountain Palace Spies (MPS) is a new spy agency that hopes to develop rapidly. However, it needs your validation in order to continue. The jewelsmiths are Clover Dianne Brook and Duala Madison March. The headquarters of MPS is located on Jaobi Hill, Pagosa Springs, Colorado, United States of America.

Sincerely, Mountain Palace Spies

Duala finished her letter and sent it to the Head of Spies, where it would be read, and they would hopefully reply with the confirmation. Two months later, they did reply, with three mice and one snow hare.

Hello Mountain Palace Spies agency,

You have been accepted in the Spybook and a mission is waiting for you in the Questbook. If you succeed in this mission, you will be an official agency and we will supply you with one student each month. Thank you for registering as an agency.

Sincerely, The Head of Spies

Duala smiled. Everything had gone almost exactly as she'd wanted it to—maybe even better.